Sia lives
on Kilimanjaro

Photographs by Anna Riwkin-Brick

Text by Astrid Lindgren

THE MACMILLAN COMPANY

NEW YORK 1959

© *1958 Rabén & Sjögren, Stockholm*

Translated from Swedish edition.

Printed in Sweden by Nordisk Rotogravyr, Stockholm 1959.

Kilimanjaro is the name of a mountain, a very high and a very beautiful mountain, one of the most beautiful in the world. Kilimanjaro is in Africa, where wild lions go hunting at night, but in the daytime, when the sun is shining on Kilimanjaro, the lions sleep peacefully.

Sia is a little girl who lives on Kilimanjaro—not right at the top, for up there is only ever-lasting snow, but farther down the slope, among banana trees and coffee bushes. Sia and her brother Sariko live in a little hut like these, with a straw roof. Her mother and father and younger brothers and sisters live there too. They belong to the Chagga people.

It is rather dark in the hut so washing is easier out of doors.
Sia has a little black and white lamb, as her own pet.

Sia is only eight years old but she can already help with all sorts of
work. Here she is cutting grass for the animals. Her little sister Linga
wants to learn how to cut grass, too, but *she* is too little—only six.

"Oh," says Sia, "how nice it would be if we had that big load of hay. If we had all that hay, we wouldn't have to work so hard and carry grass on our heads."

"I like carrying grass on my head," says Linga.

Sia's small brothers, Saika and Kitutu, want to be with Sia all
the time.

"But I can't carry both of you at the same time," says Sia.

"You can sit in this cardboard box, Kitutu, and pretend it's a boat."

"It's not a boat," says Kitutu, "it's a car."

Sia and Sariko are very fond of their kind, happy father.
"Can you guess what mother and I are going to do tomorrow?"
asks Sia's father. "We are going to the Chagga Feast at Moshi to
see King Marealle," he tells them.
"I want to go with you," says Sariko. "I do too," says Sia.
"But who will look after little Saika then?" her mother asks.
"Who will make Kitutu be good?"
"Aunt Mamole," Sia says.

"No, you are too young to go to the feast," says her father.
"Children must stay home."
The next morning mother and father set out on their journey.
"Good-bye. Look after the little ones! Don't let Linga play with
the grass knife, and see that Kitutu doesn't get lost," they say.

Sia cried a little, for she did *so* want to go to the feast. "You see that Kitutu doesn't get lost," says Sariko. "You are too small to see the King and the chiefs, Sia, but I'm not. I'm going to Moshi."

And then Sariko ran
off all by himself.
"If *he* can go,
I can, too," thinks Sia.
Sariko does not see
Sia trotting after him
over the bridge.
"I'll follow him."

"Aunt Mamole can look after the babies and I will go to Moshi to see King Marealle".

Sariko sees elephants and giraffes,
but he doesn't see Sia, for she is so small.

Someone is building a hut in the middle of the forest. It is Kifura, and Sariko knows him.

"Get me a bunch of bananas," says Kifura, "and take a couple for yourself."

Sariko uses
a long pole
with a knife
at the end
to cut the bananas.
He is glad to have
some lunch.

But now Sariko can't eat any more. He must hurry on his way.
Then he hears something behind him.

He hears someone giggling, and there is Sia.
"Sariko, I am not too young to go to look at kings and chiefs."

How angry Sariko is! "Go home," he says, "go home to Aunt Mamole and the babies. Only boys are allowed at the Chagga Feast. And it's many miles to Moshi. How do you think you will get there? You can't walk. I'm going by car," he says. "I'll get a lift."

Here comes a truck, just at the right moment.
Sariko waves to the driver, and asks for a ride.

"Climb up behind," says the driver, "and you will be in Moshi in no time at all."

"If he can ride, so can I," thinks Sia. "There will be more motor-cars. If only I dare ask for a ride! *Perhaps* I will anyway . . ."

"Please will you give me a ride?" There are lots of motor-cars on their way to Moshi today, and there are many kind drivers who understand what Sia wants, even if she does not say it out loud. Of course Sia gets a ride. And she, too, is in Moshi in a twinkling.

My, what a lot of boys there are in Moshi! What if Sariko was right

when he said that only boys were allowed at the Chagga Feast?

"Anyway, here I am, and while I am here I will see all I can," thinks Sia. "Those dancers over there look rather funny. But where is King Marealle?"

There he is! How grand he looks . . . and how kind. *He* won't be angry if one of his tiniest subjects comes to say "Good morning."
"Hello, hello!" says King Marealle. "And who are you?"
"My name is Sia," she says. "I have come a long way to see you."

"And over there is Sariko. He said I was too small to look at kings and chiefs, but I'm *not*."

"No, not at all," says King Marealle. "Perhaps I had better go and talk to Sariko, too."

"I must be dreaming," says Sia's mother who was standing in the
crowd. "It can't be Sia and Sariko talking to the King."

"I don't understand," says father. "We must have a word with them
when we get home."

"But just imagine *our* children have spoken to King Marealle," says
mother. "We will not be too cross, for they are small, and this has
been an exciting adventure."

The Chagga Feast is over. Sia is tired, and glad that
she can go home by motor-car with Sariko.

"I am not too small to look at kings and chiefs, you
see," says Sia.

"No, Sia, I guess you aren't," says Sariko. "You are
as big as Kilimanjaro."